Tales from Beyond

the

Trapdoor

GM Aaron

Grosvenor House
Publishing Limited

This book is published by
Grosvenor House Publishing Ltd
Link House
140 The Broadway, Tolworth, Surrey, KT6 7HT.
www.grosvenorhousepublishing.co.uk

This book is a work of fiction. Any resemblance to
people or events, past or present, is purely coincidental.

A CIP record for this book
is available from the British Library

ISBN 978-1-80381-423-0

Chapters

These stories have lessons to be learnt embedded in them.

Look for these lessons and enjoy reading.

All the stories are fictitious and any resemblance to any person, fact or circumstance will be a mere coincidence.

The Midnight Party

Peter was 12 years old and lived with his parents in Woodtown. He attended a boarding school in the next town, and therefore enjoyed coming home for holidays when school was on vacation. Woodtown was a small town where everyone lived in small wood and grass huts with large gardens outside their houses. Outside Peter's house, there was a hen coup where they kept a few chickens and there was also a goat tied to the large tree in the garden. When he was home for holidays, he really missed his friends and sometimes wished he did not have to come home for holidays as he had so much fun in school. He loved his family though.

Peter had two sisters called Martha and Mary. Peter's twin sisters were seven years old and kept themselves very busy by playing with their dolls all day long. So, he often found himself alone, wandering through the forest which was about 50 metres away from their house. In the forest, he liked watching the squirrels scurrying about. Some had nuts in between their teeth which they tried hard to crack while others used their tails to brush their faces. He also liked watching the monkeys swinging from tree to tree, as well as all the colourful birds singing.

Today was another one of those days when he was on holidays from boarding school and had nothing much to do. It was almost 5pm and his mother was getting supper ready. The twins were sitting outside playing with their dolls and making mud cakes. Peter told his mother he wanted to walk through the forest. 'Food will be ready soon, Peter, and you know your father wants everyone to be present when we have our supper', his mother said, without looking up and continued stirring the meat stew she was making. They were going to have the stew with rice. He liked his mother's cooking and would not miss supper for anything. Peter told his mother that he would not be long.

As he walked through the path in the forest, he looked to the right and could see the sun setting over the clearing. There were animal and bird sounds everywhere. He walked towards one of the trees that had a very low branch he often used as a seat. He sat down on the branch and started peeling the bark coming off the tree trunk. As he leaned forward to peel another loose bark coming off, he noticed that there was a light coming from a crack in the tree. He got off the branch and looked at the crack.

As he touched the crack, something that looked like a door in the tree slid to one side. Peter was very surprised. He had never seen anything like this, nor heard of sliding doors in trees. He was, however, a very brave and adventurous boy. So, he decided to investigate the tree. What he saw were stairs leading down the tree. It was quite dark in the tree so he could not see too well. The light he thought he had seen coming out of the tree had disappeared. He stood still for five minutes thinking about what to do. If he went down there, he was going to be late for supper.

Peter knew his village was very safe, so, he decided to come back to the forest after everyone was asleep in order to investigate what looked like a staircase leading down to a secret place. After marking the tree with his red felt pen, which was in his pocket, he ran home. His father had just gotten home, and they had supper. His mother and father stayed at the table after supper to talk about everything that had happened during the day and the children went to their rooms.

Peter could not wait until everyone had fallen asleep so that he could go back to the forest. He wondered what he would find in the tree. He did not want to tell anyone about his discovery because they would not believe him; and they might not let him go roaming in the forest by himself at night. Peter fell asleep dreaming about the birds and animals in the forest. He woke up with a start and looked at the clock next to his bedside table. It read 25 minutes before midnight. He tiptoed around the house. He could hear his father snoring loudly. His mother was fast asleep, as well as the twins. He did not want to go out of the house by the front door, so he slid out of his window, jumped onto the ground, and ran quickly towards the forest. Luckily for him, the moon was out, and it shone its bright light along the foot path.

After a few minutes, Peter found the tree he had marked with his pen, but he made a note to himself to bring his flashlight, the next time, he had any midnight adventures. Just as he was about to touch the tree, the door slid aside, and he could see the stairs leading down the tree. Peter hesitated for a moment before he got into the tree and walked down the stairs. The inside of the tree was brightly lit. As he walked down the stairs, he could hear music and laughter. When Peter got to the bottom of the stairs, he could see a clearing ahead of him. There were large trees that were brightly decorated with Christmas lights of all colours. There were also tables laden with foods of all kinds: fried chicken, meat, and roast pork chops, shrimps, fruit and vegetable salad. However, what caught his attention were the people dancing around the trees. He had read about fairies, gnomes and elves. He did not think they existed.

'Oh look', someone shouted and pointed towards him, we have a human visitor. 'Don't look so surprised!' A fairy dancing above him said. She explained that there was always a party at midnight and that all the gnomes, elves and fairies came together to have a good time. Peter was very shocked. He was tempted to grab a piece of chicken but stopped himself. He must remember his manners, he thought to himself. Before he could think of anything else, one of the elves pulled him into the dancing circle. And after some introductions of Peter – the newcomer – to everyone present, Peter and the elves, danced and danced all night long, only stopping for a few minutes to have something to eat and drink and then continued dancing. He made friends with all of them. They asked him to come back the next day. He was not very sure about coming back but he had enjoyed himself. The party went on until the early hours of the morning.

Suddenly, just before the first rays of the sun shone, everything disappeared. Peter was left standing in the deserted clearing. The fairies, gnomes and elves were all gone. 'Hello, hello! Where has everyone disappeared to?' There was no response. He quickly run up the stairs and run all the way home. He was hoping his father was not outside smoking his pipe very early in the morning as he did sometimes. Fortunately for him, his father was not up yet. He pulled himself up his window and jumped into bed and fell asleep, dreaming of the party. When he woke up, his parents had gone to work, and his sisters were playing outside with their dolls as usual. They invited Peter to come and play with them and offered him some 'tea' and mud cakes. He played with them for a while, and then went back into the house daydreaming about the previous night.

Had he dreamt the whole thing, or had it happened? He wondered. The day went by very quickly and it was nightfall. His parents came home; the family had dinner and soon everyone was asleep. Peter waited until it was 11pm and he ran quickly into the forest. When he got to where the tree was there was no light shining from the crack in the tree trunk. Peter was confused but he decided to wait for a while. At midnight, the door in the tree slid open and he realised that the party started only at midnight. As before, he ran down the stairs into the clearing and just as before, there were dancing fairies, elves and gnomes everywhere. There were tables laden with food and drink.

Just before the first rays of light from the sun appeared, one of the fairies took him aside and told him not to let anyone know about their secret. 'If you tell anyone about the midnight party, we will not be able to use this tree for our parties anymore'. Peter promised to keep the secret and went home after everything had vanished. Once again, no one was awake when he got home, and he went directly to bed. When he woke up, he went down to the kitchen and had some milk and bread.

Now what Peter did not know was that the twins had come into his room one night when he was sleeping, and saw that Peter had sweets and biscuits stuffed in his jacket. They also noticed that Peter's shoes were soiled with very white sand. They made up their minds to find out where Peter got the goodies from and why his shoes had that colour of sand on them because the sand around their house was dark brown. 'We could use this sand to make more mud cakes and they will be a beautiful colour', Martha had said to Mary. They did not question Peter about anything, but to keep a close eye on him for the rest of the day. When it was nightfall, the twins went to bed as usual but pretended to fall asleep.

When Peter left the house and ran towards the forest, the twins were close behind making sure that Peter did not suspect he was being followed. They were beginning to feel frightened as Peter kept leading them deep into the forest. At one point, Martha thought she saw a snake and nearly screamed. When Peter got to the clearing, he went through the secret door as usual, descended the stairs and joined everyone else dancing. The twins were very surprised that Peter had entered the tree. 'Should we follow him? I have never seen a tree with a door'. Mary was frightened, but Martha pushed her towards the tree.

When they got to the tree, they pushed the trunk slightly, and went down the stairs. The moment they got to where the party was, everything froze. The fairies, gnomes and elves froze, and then vanished with the light and the table that had been laid with food. Peter had not seen the twins come down the tree, but when everything froze, he turned around to find out what had happened. 'Martha! Mary! What are you doing here?' 'We knew you always went somewhere at night, so we decided to follow you', the girls said, a bit ashamed for being found out. 'Because of you, my friends have disappeared forever'. Peter was very angry, but he did not want to shout at the twins and make them cry because he was worried, they might tell their parents and then he would be in big trouble. He led them out of the forest and towards the house. They spoke very little and went to sleep.

After that fateful evening when everything had disappeared, Peter went into the forest night after night hoping, the sliding door would appear, and he would be able go down to the party again; but he waited in vain. Because the secret of the fairy folk had been discovered, they had gone to the forest in the next town and Peter never saw them again during his holidays. Peter went back to boarding school with a feeling of having enjoyed his holidays even though his midnight party was gone for good.

One day, when Peter was sleeping at night in school, he thought he heard a noise coming from underneath his bed. He bent down and looked under the bed. He saw a trapdoor with light coming from underneath it. He opened the trapdoor and lo and behold! There were stairs leading down the trapdoor. He knew what he would find there as he descended the stairs with a smile on his face. And so, it was that Peter had discovered the midnight party again.

The House of Sweets

Once upon a time, in the village of Tapeh, lived a small family of four: a mother, a father and their two sons. They were poor but had enough to eat from day to day. The father was a hunter and brought home deer meat or birds he had shot with his catapult. The mother did not work because she was kept busy with housework and taking care of the family. She also liked working in the garden. The garden was divided into two parts. On one half which was directly in front of the house, she planted lovely flowers like roses, daffodils, and tulips. On the other half, which was directly behind the flowers, she planted crops like sweet potatoes, yams and leaves they could use as additional ingredients for cooking. All in all, they were happy from day to day.

They were different from the rest of the people in the village because, most of the people were rich. It was not unusual for a resident to have two or three houses and to wear beautiful clothes. The husbands worked in the city and bought their families beautiful clothes and other gifts. The people of the village were polite to the Sawyer family, but they were not included in activities like parties and festival celebrations, because they were thought to be different, and just would not fit in. The father and mother worried about this sometimes because they wanted their children to have friends and feel included in the village activities. However, the father always believed that one day, they would be accepted by everyone in the village even though he did not know how this would happen.

One day, as he was about to shoot a deer, he accidentally turned the arrow towards himself, and the arrow entered his arm. He howled in pain as he walked home. As he walked towards the house, his wife heard him shouting and came to him quickly. She helped him into the house and pulled the arrow out and dressed the wound. However, he could not use his arm. Days passed, and the wound on his arm was getting worse. It was not healing properly.

The family became sad because they did not have any meat to eat with their soup and as the boys were only eight and nine years old, they were not allowed to hunt for meat in the forest. The mother did not know where their next meal was coming from because the crops in the garden were not doing so well. The Sawyer family, however, were too proud to ask for help from their fellow villagers. They did not want anyone feeling sorry for them. So it was that day after day, the father's arm got worse and worse, and the family was about to have their last meal that evening.

The two boys sat quietly together wondering what they should do. Just before their evening meal, they told their mother they were going for a walk in the woods. They were hardly allowed to walk in the woods just before sunset. Their mother was so distracted that she agreed to their request and told them to make sure they were on time for supper. Their father did not hear them going as he was always sleeping because of the pain in his arm. The two boys walked through the woods stopping now and again to pick some nuts and fruits. One of them thought he saw a deer and even though they did not know how they were going to catch it, they started running after it. They had almost got the deer by the tail when it ran off even further into the forest. It was past sunset now. It was getting darker. The moon was out and shone brightly on the forest floor.

The boys were determined to take something home so that their parents would be proud of them, so they kept running deeper and deeper into the forest. As they ran through the forest, the trees got less and less until they reached the end of the forest. They were about to turn back when they saw a house. They decided to go closer because it seemed to be glowing. When they got quite close to the house, they could see that the house had all kinds of sweets hanging from the windows and around the doors. The boys were so excited. Why not? Every child liked sweets.

They were just about to pull a long green and white candy down when the door opened and an old woman with long white hair opened the door. 'Don't be rude', she frowned as she spoke. 'You must always ask before you take anything from anyone'. The boys were too surprised to speak because they were staring at the old woman with white hair and red shining eyes. She was wearing a long white dress, big earrings and white sandals. As they entered the house, there were sweets everywhere: on the tables, walls, and floor.

'It's about time you boys came. I have been waiting for three years for you to come and collect my sweet creation'.

'Three years! Why? You don't even know us'. The boys said in amazement.

'I know all about you. I know how you are not accepted in the village because you are not as rich as everyone else. I know that your father got hurt in the forest, and I know that right now, at this very minute, if you do not hurry up home with these sweets, your mother will die from worry because you have been away from home for three hours. So, take these sweets home to your parents and sell them to the villagers. You will have enough money for whatever you want to do as a family. I must warn you. Do not tell anyone about this place. I am a witchdoctor. Witchdoctors are not well liked in the village'.

The boys took two big bags of sweets home to their parents and promised the woman to come back for more when they were out of sweets. She made them promise not to tell anyone about where she lived. They were to come back by themselves for more sweets and keep her location a secret from everyone.

The boys agreed to keep her place a secret from everyone even their parents and rushed home, dragging the two big bags of sweets with them. When they got home, their mother was waiting outside for them. She was very worried. After scolding her sons for coming home late, she noticed the two big bags they had next to them on the floor. She asked them what they contained. The boys asked her if their father was awake because they wanted to tell them some good news together. After a few minutes, the whole family was in one room and the boys told their parents about the gypsy woman and her house of sweets, but they told their parents that they were warned by the witchdoctor not to tell anyone, including them about where her house was. They did not know what would happen when everyone else knew where her house was.

Their parents were so happy. They could now afford to take their father to the hospital to have his wounded arm treated. They would be able to get enough money from selling the sweets and would move into a bigger house; buy good clothes and enjoy life just like the other rich villagers did. So it was that the Sawyer family that everyone had rejected because they had no money became rich overnight.

When the father's arm had healed properly, the parents took the sweets to the village centre, built a large shed and started selling the sweets. The villagers had never seen so many sweets in their lives. These were no ordinary sweets. They were of different shapes, sizes and colours. Every morning after that, one of the parents took turns to go to the village centre to sell their sweets. The other parent took sweets to the next town to sell to the people there. They had a lot of money from these sweets and moved into a bigger house with a larger garden.

They had a big chicken coup and some farm animals in a big shed behind their house. People in the village started respecting them because they were not poor anymore. The children played with the other children in the village and had small, sweet parties in their house. Their parents went into the village centre for festivals and other functions and made friends with everyone.

What everyone did not understand was where the family had got the sweets from and how they could get rich overnight. There was a man who was very jealous of the family because they were almost as rich as he was. He decided to find out where the family got the sweets from. Meanwhile, the boys always went to the woman in the forest, every two weeks for sweets. They always had tea and cakes before they left and told her stories of what was happening in the village. On one of these occasions when the boys went to the witchdoctor's house, the parents were arguing amongst themselves as to how they could find out where the boys got the sweets from. 'You know you can't follow them to the forest. They were warned not to tell anyone about where she lives!' The mother shouted angrily. 'I know! But we must know where they go to. What kind of parents are we? Letting our children go off to some witchdoctor's house every fortnight without knowing where exactly she lives?!' The father argued. And so, the argument went on.

The jealous villager who wanted to find out where the family got their sweets happened to be passing by the house at that time and he stopped and listened to everything they said. He smiled to himself and walked off with a plan forming in his mind. And so it happened that on the day the boys were going to the witchdoctor's house to get more sweets for their parents to sell, the wicked villager who wanted to know where the family got their sweets from, followed the boys through the forest to the house where the woman lived. The boys had no idea they had been followed. Had they known, they would have turned around and gone back to the house because they knew how important it was for their secret to be kept.

People in those days were wary of witchdoctors and fortune tellers. As usual, the boys sat outside the house and had some tea and cakes with the mysterious woman. They told her stories about the village and how the sweets had changed their lives. All this while, nobody knew the man was listening to their every word and was hiding behind a large oak tree near the window. After the boys left the woman's house with the bags of sweets as usual, the man sprung onto them just as they were coming out of the forest. 'Give me the bags', he ordered. The boys did not know what to say so they gave him the bags and ran home crying. The man laughed all the way home. He thought about all the money he would gain from selling the sweets. He decided to have his supper before opening the bags. In this way, he would have all the time in the world to examine each sweet. As he lived alone, he was not worried about anybody disturbing or distracting him from his task.

The greedy man had his supper, smiling to himself all the while. After that he went into his room and took the bags out. He dipped his hand in to bring out a sweet. All he got was a stone. He looked into the bag. All the sweets had changed into stones because the only ones who should open the bag of sweets was the Sawyer family. Unfortunately, all the sweets the villagers bought changed into stones at the same time the ones in the bag had changed.

The next day, all the villagers matched to the house of the Sawyer family and shouted and threw sticks at their house. They were very angry. Suddenly, everyone in the village hated the Sawyer family. The Sawyer family were angry too because when the boys went back to see the woman in the forest. Her house had disappeared and there was evidence that she had ever lived there. It was as if she had disappeared into thin air. The Sawyer family were now hated in the village.

It became clear to them that they were not liked for who they were, but for what they could give the villagers: sweets. They also realised that had it not been for the selling of sweets which provided them with money to buy nice things, they would never have been accepted by the villagers.

One night when everyone was asleep, they packed their bags, took the money they had and left their old town for another town. They travelled in their horse and carriage, in silence and as they were nearing the town they were going to, they stopped in the middle of the road suddenly! In the middle of the road, on the floor, sat the white-haired woman. 'Oh, what long faces you have. All this was a lesson to show you that people must accept you for who you are and not for riches or objects. Here, take these bags of sweets. They should be enough to sell for a long time. I am going back to the land of my ancestors because my work here is done'. After saying that, she disappeared into thin air.

The Sawyers settled in a new town. Over here, the people were friendly and accepted them just as they were. Even though their new trade of selling sweets did not make them any richer than they already were, they had enough to eat and drink for a long time.

The children went to the local school and made friends with the other children and the parents were invited to all the activities in the town hall. They were very happy in the end.

On the Bendy Road to Happily Ever After

The Kingdom of Nassa was very beautiful. The people were very happy and loved their King and Queen. However, their only child was very spoilt. Her parents gave her everything she wanted. Princess Awisi had always dreamt of getting married one day and dressed her dolls in wedding gowns most of the time.

When she was 18, the Princess told her parents that she was ready for marriage.

'You are too young!' The King shouted in alarm.

'No!' Princess Awisi shouted.

'I just want to get married and live happily ever after'. The Princess said as she stamped her feet.

For once, the Queen, her mother, was at a loss for words.

The King had meetings with his advisors and asked them to send messengers to the various Kingdoms in the search of a Prince. In a few days, all the messengers came back and told the King that none of the Princes wanted to marry her because they had heard she was so spoilt.

In another Kingdom, a Prince was making plans to win the Princess' hand in marriage. In the Kingdom of Basemi, Prince Asem, had heard of how beautiful Princess Awisi was.

'Beautiful but spoilt, Sir'. His servant said to him, as they walked around his courtyard.

'Really? Well, I have decided to marry her'. The prince said to his servant.

They exchanged a knowing look and then both men broke down in fits of laughter. They had a plan.

And so, it was, that the Prince of Basemi married the beautiful Princess Awisi in her kingdom.

It was a long journey to the prince's kingdom. The Princess felt so sleepy.

As the Prince and Princess got to Basemi, the Prince held her hand and smiled at her kindly.

'But where are the people who should be welcoming us?' Princess Awisi asked.

She had thought there would be people all lined up by the roadside leading to the prince's castle.

The carriage went through the small kingdom, passing along narrow roads, going past hills and valleys and eventually stopping in a clearing.

Princess Awisi looking out of the carriage exclaimed:

'But it is only a small hut!'

'Yes, this is our home, my fair Princess'. The prince said whilst helping Princess Awisi out of the carriage.

'My goodness!' Princess Awisi held her throat and seemed to gasp for air. 'But where are the servants?'

'There will be no servants, my dear. You will have to do everything. My parents died leaving me with nothing, but a title and this small house. The prince explained.

His servant left after he took her luggage into the house.

'But you lied to me! I hate you!' The Princess screamed as she sat on a chair so old it shook under her weight.

'This is your new life!' The prince retorted as he left the house slamming the door behind him.

After he had left, Princess Awisi looked around her: a little cottage with two rooms, one small sofa and a rickety bed. Unbelievable!

The Princess knew she could not go back to her parents' castle.

Every morning, the prince helped Princess Awisi make breakfast and clean the house before he went out to work. For the first few days, she refused to speak to him, but after a week, she found that she enjoyed doing the chores and even started singing whilst she did them.

'So how is your new bride doing?' The servant asked the Prince.

'Surprisingly, she is doing very well. She is getting used to her new home. It might be time for the task'. The Princess had settled in her new home, albeit, reluctantly. The Prince and Princess had been married for four weeks now.

'Oh yes, the task...' The servant said, thoughtfully.

The prince came home one evening and put a sack of little green bananas on the floor. They landed on the floor with a loud thud! Princess Awisi ran out of her little room where she had been mending one of her skirts.

'What are those?' She asked, pointing at the small green bananas scattered all over the floor.

'There is a shortage of food in town so we can only have these green bananas for dinner'. He replied.

'But I don't know how to peel green bananas?' Princess Awisi wailed.

The prince raised one eyebrow, looked at the Princess, and then went out again.

The Princess sat down on the floor and covered her face with her hands and cried.

Life seemed to be so hard.

After crying for a long while, she got up and started walking around the bananas, whilst wondering how she was going to remove the green peels wrapped tightly around each banana.

'You really must sit down you know. Going around in circles won't solve anything. Take a knife and make a long deep mark along each banana. It will be easier to take the peel off', the voice said.

Princess Awisi looked around.

'I know I heard a small voice!' She said aloud.

She thought she had imagined the voice. She sat down and then saw something like a butterfly, hopping from one banana onto another.

'What . . . it can't be? You cannot be real! A fairy?!'

'But, of course, Awisi. Don't be silly! The prince will soon be here. Get to work!' After Awisi had calmed down, the fairy demonstrated how Awisi could get the peels off each banana.

So, the Princess prepared their dinner after peeling all the bananas and cooking them. She also made a nice chicken gravy sauce to go with it. When the Prince came, he was very surprised. After they had eaten, he took hold of the Princess' hands and swirled her into a dance. He was so pleased. In his head, he sang: 'She has passed the test!!! She is truly my wife!' Other Princesses had failed the test and had ran away.

The Princess had never seen the prince so happy.

'My Prince! We are here!' The servant called out. It had been a long ride from the Princess's Kingdom to the Prince's Palace.

The Princess woke up with a start.

Awisi sat up abruptly and looked around her. The Prince sat across from her, looking at her, curiously. They had arrived at his Kingdom.

'Are you alright?' He asked because he could see she was frightened.

Princess Awisi looked down at the hands and her clothes. She was still dressed in her beautiful, white, sparkly gown. Her ring was throwing little lights around the carriage, so her wedding had not been a dream.

But, what about what had happened after the wedding? Had that been a dream? The poor home of the prince, the numerous bananas she had peeled and the fairy who had who had helped her.

The servant was outside the door of the carriage and was still waiting to be given orders to open the door. The Princess looked out of her window. There were people lined up on the street and outside the palace, waving and cheering.

She got up and walked along the street towards the palace. The prince was next to her holding her hand and waving. They got to the entrance of the palace, the Princess was just about to dismiss her experience as a dream when she saw a little flutter over the prince's shoulder.

It was the little fairy who had helped her peel all those bananas to prepare dinner in her dream!

The Princess gasped and caught the prince's eye.

He winked at her.

He knows! She thought to herself. The Princess had passed the task of peeling all those green bananas for dinner. She knew that green banana peels were so hard to remove.

Along the streets of the Kingdom everyone cheered the Prince and Princess as they entered the palace.

The Prince and Princess lived happily ever after in their palace. She got the kind of life she wanted, but she appreciated this and was no longer proud and snobbish.

Now, what would have happened to the Princess' fairy-tale marriage to the Prince, if she had not been able to peel all those green bananas for dinner?

These were her thoughts, as she held on tightly to the Prince's arm, as they walked steadly towards their castle.

Princess Lizzybelle

Once upon a time, in a town where there was only happiness, peace and love, ruled a king and queen. Their subjects were treated fairly and lived in beautiful houses. They had plenty to eat and drink, and they were well looked after by their king and queen. The palace was in the middle of the kingdom and the houses of their people were scattered all around the palace. The king and queen were happy, but sometimes, they cried together because they had no child.

They would often sit near the palace windows where they would watch the children run around the palace gardens, shouting out at each other in their games.

It was very hard for the King and Queen because what they wanted most, was a child of their own. The king would comfort his wife and tell her to be patient and that in time, they would have a child. The Queen would then dab her eyes with her silk perfumed handkerchief and plaster a smile on her face whilst waving to the children, below the castle window.

A whole year had gone by since the king and queen had married in a big and beautiful wedding, that had been talked about for many months after. There had been many guests from far and wide. The wedding had been attended by Kings, Queens, Princes and Princesses. And now, everyone was anticipating the good news of the future heir or heiress for the kingdom.

One morning, the queen was standing by one of the windows of the palace watching the people of the kingdom going about their businesses. The men were very hardworking: they were mostly hunters, fishermen and traders. The wives were also very hardworking. When their husbands went to work, they went to the river side and fetched water for their cooking and washing. After that most of them went to their friends' houses to have their long hair woven into braids. Some of them sat in front of their houses and brushed their hair out and just watched the children play. And so, it was that when the queen was at one of her windows watching everything that was happening that morning, a message was delivered to her by a messenger that she was to go to the forest to a certain meeting place. Someone who knew the 'problem' she was having wanted to see her. The only problem she knew she had and which everyone knew about was the fact that she could not have a child. She told the messenger to tell the person she will be there by mid-afternoon. She did not want the king to know where she was going and therefore decided not to say anything.

After lunch with the king, the queen told him she was going riding. 'Won't you take a lady- in -waiting with you?' 'No, I will be back soon. I just want to go for a nice ride by myself. It will give me time to think'. 'Ok', the king said. He did not want to argue with the queen. He understood the queen was sad from time to time because they did not have a child. The queen went to the stables and had her favourite horse saddled for her. She got on the horse and rode towards the forest where she was meeting the person. On her way through the forest, she admired the beauty of the greenery. The birds were flying and animals were scurrying around.

Twenty minutes after the start of her journey through the forest, she got to the tree house where the person was. As she tied the horse to a tree, a woman came out of the tree house. She had one eye in the centre of her head. She had long dreadlocked white hair and wore white clothes. The queen was a bit frightened to see the woman and moved backwards immediately. 'Your royal highness, you are very welcome to my house', the woman said as she climbed down the tree house using the stairs next to the tree. When she reached the bottom of the tree, she bowed down to the queen. The queen quickly told her to stand up and asked her why she had sent for her. 'Well, I know you have been trying to have a child for some time and I have a solution for you. Come up to my house'.

The queen looked around nervously, but she decided to follow the woman up the stairs to the house. When they got to the house, the queen noticed that there were pots of clay of different colours near the window. There were no flowers in the pots as one would have expected. The house was very tidy with only one table and chair and a bed at the far corner of the room.

The queen sat down on the only chair in the room, and waited for the woman to tell her what she was waiting to hear.

'I can help you have a child. As you can see, I have clay in pots near the window. I will make a child out of clay. No one must know that you did not give birth to the child. Not even the king. Here, take this and cover your stomach with it. Then wear your clothes over them. Everyone will think you are pregnant. When you are in your ninth month of 'pregnancy', mind you, we are pretending you are pregnant, come back for the baby'.

With that, the woman stood up, and gave the queen some items in a bag and told her it was time to leave. The queen quickly went downstairs, mounted her horse, and rode quickly out of the forest and to the palace. When she got to the palace, the king was by the window looking out for her for she had spent almost three hours away from home. She told him, she had to help some villagers along the way, so she could not come home as quickly as she wanted to. The queen went into her chambers and peered into the bag containing the items the woman had given her. There was a bottle of quick invisible glue and the new 'stomach' she had to stick on her stomach. The woman told her that once she stuck the new stomach on, it would keep growing so there would be no need to take it off.

After a month, the queen told the king she was expecting a child and they were very excited. The king and queen were very happy and looking forward to having a baby in the palace. Day after day, the queen's stomach grew larger with her child.

Every day in the kingdom, people talked about the arrival of the new prince or princess. A month before the baby's arrival, the queen went back to see the old woman. She gave the queen something to drink and went to the windowsill and took out some brown clay and started moulding a baby out of it. The queen was surprised at how fast the woman worked at making the clay come to life. She then touched the queen's stomach and the 'clay baby' immediately went into the stomach. Then the woman said quietly, 'If you follow my instructions, the baby will grow up to be a normal baby and be like everyone else. No one must know that he or she was made from clay. The child must never stand too close to fire.

This is very important. I do not know what will happen when the child disobeys this instruction, but these are the instructions you must follow. You must never come here again because my work here is done'. And with this, she disappeared into thin air together with the tree house and all her pots of clay. The queen was left standing there in shock. She quickly rode out of the forest.

After a month, the queen gave birth to a bouncing baby girl called Jizzybelle. Jizzybelle was a very beautiful girl. The king and queen were very fond of her and gave her everything she wanted. She had a room full of dolls, a wardrobe full of little gowns and hats. At seven years old, she had everything she could ever want from her parents. She was very happy. The queen made sure that the little princess was never too close to the fireplace when the palace was being warmed and not too close to pots cooking on the fire when she sometimes went to the kitchen to watch the servants making food for the king and queen. The king noticed that the queen always panicked when Jizzybelle went near a burning fire. Strangely, Jizzybelle was fascinated by fire and always wanted to go close to watch the sparks that flew from the logs burning. But she also knew her mother did not want her too near the fire, so she always stood away from it and watched.

Unknown to the queen there was someone who worked in the kitchen who was a woman. The woman did not like Jizzybelle from the first day she laid eyes on her and planned to destroy her. She just did not how she would accomplish this until the day Jizzybelle came into the kitchen. She noticed how Jizzybelle stood very far away from the kitchen fire while watching it. She wondered why she did not get close enough to watch the sparks flying. 'Jizzy, get closer to the fire. Don't you want to get warmer?' she asked, with a smirk on her face. Jizzybelle shrunk back. The woman terrified her anyway. She had two big front teeth that reminded her of an angry rabbit. She ran back to her room to play with her dolls.

Because the queen was afraid of what might happen to Jizzybelle, she did not allow her to have any friends. The queen was afraid that someone might push Jizzybelle into a fire by mistake. She had nightmares about this every night. She often tossed and turned in bed which made the king wonder why even with such a beautiful daughter his wife was still not as happy as she should have been. She was always worried about Jizzybelle. The queen had still not told the king how it was that they had a daughter. He had no reason to believe that Jizzybelle was not like other children. Besides, she had promised the woman in the forest to keep it a secret.

Jizzybelle often went to play at the edge of the forest with a maid from the palace. One day, she wanted to play in the forest, but the maid was nowhere to be found. It was a cold winter day. The sun was shining but it was still very cold. She put on her favourite coat and ran to the forest to the spot where she and the maid normally played. Meanwhile, the evil woman from the kitchen saw her leave the palace and followed her. She decided to put her plan into action. She waited until Jizzybelle was tired from playing and went to her from her hiding place in the forest. 'Jizzy, I have some warm milk and cookies in my house which is just close by. Why don't you come for a little snack? After that we can walk back to the palace'.

Jizzybelle was a bit hungry, so she followed the woman who led her into a hut nearby and gave her some cookies. The weather was still very cold, so she lit a fire. Jizzybelle started feeling very uncomfortable. She started feeling very strange and hot. She put her hand to her face to wipe the sweat and some clay-like sand came off. Poor Jizzybelle had begun to melt! Before the woman could reach her side, Princess Jizzybelle had melted into thick clay in the middle the floor. The woman panicked and started to cry. She had not expected this to happen. She ran to the palace for help.

All day, the queen had a feeling that something bad was about to happen, but she did not know what it was. Now when she saw the woman running towards the palace with her hands above her head screaming for help, she knew that something had happened to her dear daughter Jizzybelle.

The woman explained what had happened. She said Jizzybelle was cold, and she just told her to go to her house and have a glass of milk and cookies. She said she had no idea that Jizzybelle would melt. The queen was very sad. She asked the king to banish the woman from their kingdom. She cried for days and days on end. She would go to Jizzybelle's room and play with her toys and not come out for hours. The king was very worried because the queen would not eat, and she had become very pale over the past few weeks.

One day, the queen decided to go to the forest to look for the woman who gave her the child. It so happened that the woman knew she would come and was waiting for her. She asked the queen to come to the forest the next day with the king. The next day, both the king and the queen went to the forest to see the old woman. Magically, the tree house had appeared again with the pots of clay. The woman went to one of the pots, sang a song and out came Jizzybelle from one of the pots.

The king was very amazed. He knew the secret now. The woman gave them Jizzybelle, who was asleep, and told them to take her back to the palace and take care of her, with the same instructions never to let her anywhere near fire. In the meantime, the woman said no one in the village would remember what had happened to the princess and Jizzybelle would grow into a nice woman if she was well protected. The king and queen promised to do just that and went to the palace where all three lived happily ever after.

Rabbit Girl

'Amina! Amina! Where are you?!' yelled her mother.

Amina could hear her mother's voice from where she sat, at the edge of the forest. The family's house was on the outskirts of the village. They lived very close to the forest and the main river, that ran through the village. On most evenings, when Amina had finished her chores, she could often be found seated, cross-legged, on a large rock, and just staring ahead of her. Amina's mother knew her daughter was a dreamer. She would often come home after her time on her favourite rock and would talk about the animals and birds she had seen.

Amina was known to spin interesting stories about things she had seen around her. She had gone to her favourite spot in the late afternoon. Amina had discovered this rock by accident after she had stumbled on it whilst skipping around the grass. The grass around the flat rock had been quite long, and Amina had not seen the rock and had tripped on the rock. The shape of the rock was like a mushroom and from then on, was a good place for Amina to sit on.

On this evening, Amina was jolted out of her dreams, or maybe what she thought she had seen had not been a dream. Her mother's voice pierced through the air. Amina quickly got off the rock and ran towards home. Her mother was standing at the entrance of the compound. 'Amina! You should have been here half an hour ago. We should have started cooking supper a while ago'.

'Sorry, Mama. I will help you now'.

'It's alright, I am nearly done. Help me give Mami a bath before supper'.

At eight years old, Amina was a great help to her mother. She helped her with the general chores after school, and also helped with taking care of Mami, her little sister, who was nearly 2 years old. Soon, supper was served, and as they all sat around the table, today, Amina could not focus on her father's tales of his work in the city. She was distracted by what she thought she had seen in the forest, as she had sat on her favourite rock.

In the distance, Amina had seen an opening in the clearing ahead of her. The sand on top, and around the opening, had started to bubble, as if something was pushing its way through it. Amina had not been able to tear her eyes away from what she was seeing. The hole in the ground continued to choke out sand, and then, out jumped, a huge rabbit. The rabbit shook the sand off, and her ears twitched madly. Amina had been transfixed whilst she watched the events unfold.

The next few minutes were very shocking for Amina. The rabbit had stretched to its full height, whilst on tiptoe, and suddenly, its fur started rolling off its body from the top. After a few minutes, Amina watched a girl with a full head of curly black hair step away from the fur. The girl bent down and rolled the fur neatly, and carefully, put it under a short bush for safe keeping. She then started to skip and run around the clearing for about an hour. She would bend down and pick up some flowers, and stick these in her hair, or she would pick some flowers and sit down cross-legged whilst trying to arrange them into a bouquet. After some time, when the sun had begun to set, she looked up, appeared to panic, and then went to where she had stretched the fur. She put the fur on the floor and lay on top of it – her head aligning with where the head should be, and her back aligning with where her short tail would be. Amina saw the fur cover the girl, and in a flash, she became a rabbit again, and burrow down the hole. Amina had been in great shock. How could a rabbit become a girl? Amina had then rushed home as she heard her mother calling her.

'Amina, you are very quiet today'. Her father observed.

'I am fine, father'. Amina said with a smile. 'I am just listening to your stories'. Amina was also making a mental note to go back to the forest the next day. She had to see 'Rabbit Girl' again.

It had been raining for the past three days so Amina could not go out into the forest. She was very curious about the girl she called 'Rabbit Girl', and she wanted to see her again. After five days, the rain had finally stopped completely but it took another three days for the ground to completely dry up. It was the day after market day, and there was not much to be done around the house. The family had had breakfast, and were indoors, relaxing. Amina told her parents she was going for a walk. The weather was nice, on this bright mid-morning.

There was a light breeze and Amina skipped along the path leading to her spot near the edge of the forest. She brushed some leaves off her favourite rock and sat down. She gazed towards the rabbit hole. After nearly an hour, Amina got tired of waiting for the rabbit to come out of the hole and got up and stretched. She decided to start walking towards the hole so she could to have a little peek. As she walked close to the hole, she could see ripples around the hole. The rabbit was coming out! Amina thought. She ran and hid behind one of the trees near the clearing.

As she had seen before, the sand around the hole appeared to splutter, and out, shot the rabbit! Rabbit girl shook the sand off her and stretched to her full height. Her fur fell off, and as she had done before she rolled the fur neatly, so she could make sure it was safe. But then she started walking towards Amina, who had been watching the whole thing in awe. The girl had wanted to put the rolled-up fur, behind the tree Amina was hiding at.

'What do I do, what do I do?' Amina thought to herself, as she watched Rabbit

Girl get closer and closer, with each step she took.

Before Rabbit Girl got close to her, Amina decided to jump from behind the tree.

'Hey!' Amina said.

'Whaa...who are you'? Rabbit Girl pointed at Amina, looking at her cautiously, and looking beyond Amina to see if there was anyone else around. 'You know, I saw you the last time you were here. I have been wondering when I will see you again'.

'Oh?' Amina said. 'So, how come you are the way you are?'

'What do you mean?'. Rabbit Girl asked, with a sly smile on her face. She turned to Amina and said: 'Oh, you mean, why I am a rabbit as well as a human girl. Come, sit next to me, and let me tell you what had happened'.

Amina and Rabbit Girl walked towards one of the trees that had thick branches that provided shade from the sun and sat underneath the tree.

Rabbit Girl begun her story:

One night, a few months ago, she had come out of the rabbit hole for some fresh air when her family had gone to bed. There had been a full moon and she had been very fixated on the stars that had been sprinkled around the moon, as well as across the sky. She then saw something flickering across the sky and had followed it with her gaze. Then suddenly, a golden ball shot through the sky, coming towards her, and then landed next to her with a thud.

'Oh!' Rabbit Girl had said as she realised that the golden ball was a fairy girl sitting next to her.

'I will grant you any wish'. The fairy girl had said after the Rabbit had overcome her shock.

The Rabbit asked fairy girl to be able to become human, so she could see how humans lived by going into the village.

'Very well . . . but there is only one thing you should be careful of when I grant you this wish'.

But before the rabbit (now Rabbit Girl) could find out what she needed to be cautious about, now that her wish had been granted, Fairy Girl had disappeared leaving behind a trail of gold dust that disappeared above the trees in the forest.

Amina was very intrigued by Rabbit Girl's story.

'So, you do not know what it is you need to be cautious about?'

'No. But I have been having fun being a girl. I have been to the marketplace, and other areas in the village. I have seen you from a distance'.

'Oh, you have!'

Amina and Rabbit Girl talked for a bit longer, until the sun begun to set, and Amina had to go back home.

Amina watched Rabbit Girl as she lay down on the full length of her fur and was subsequently engulfed in it. The rabbit then scurried down the hole, towards her home and her family. Amina quickly turned away and ran home, with thoughts of Rabbit Girl, on her mind.

What Amina did not know was that as soon as she got home, the rabbit came out of the hole again, and transformed in a girl. Rabbit Girl looked towards Amina's home with longing. Rabbit Girl had a secret. She had always wanted to be fully human and was thinking about how she could achieve this. The Rabbit had lied to Amina about having a family down in the rabbit hole. The truth was she had been separated from her family when she had been born and had found herself all alone. She had had to survive throughout her life. She would come out for food, stretch a bit and would go back into her hole. She was very lonely and had no friends. Every day, Rabbit Girl would always come out of her rabbit hole and stare at the human folk. She wanted to be part of a human family, and it was during one of these times, that the fairy girl had found her and had granted her the wish of being human, sometimes. Now, Rabbit Girl wanted to be human, forever. She would have to think of a plan.

The next day, when Amina came back to the rabbit hole, little did she know that today's events were going to change her life. Rabbit Girl had come out of the rabbit hole and had transformed into a human. She and Amina had played games and had also enjoyed chasing each other in and out of the forest. Then Rabbit Girl said to Amina: 'You should touch my rabbit fur that is spread out, behind that tree. Go on, lie on it. It is so soft'.

Amina skipped towards the rabbit fur, and laid out it, just as she had seen Rabbit Girl do. Suddenly, the fur started to engulf

Amina. She tried to shake it off but failed. Her last human thought was that of disappointment as she watched Rabbit Girl run away from her.

Rabbit Girl thought of how she was now rid of the fur, which she viewed as a curse.

Amina, now a Rabbit, run towards her house. But she could not go into her compound, as she feared she would be chased out of the house. Of course, her parents could not have known she was now a rabbit.

The fairy who had given Rabbit Girl the gift of transforming into a girl had observed everything that had happened. She shook her head in disappointment. She had thought Rabbit Girl would be happy with being human, at least some of the time.

She watched Rabbit Girl, now a normal girl, go all around town. She was very happy and tried all the things she had wanted to do.

But Amina the rabbit was very sad. She did not want to go into the rabbit hole. She just wanted to go home, but unfortunately, she could not. From a distance, she watched her mother stand in front of the door, worried, and looking from left to right.

Then it begun to rain.

Amina started to shake as the rain drops permeated through her fur. She wanted to cry. She was scared and terrified that she will remain a rabbit forever. Amina did not see the fairy fluttering above her and pouring some gold dust on her. Suddenly, the fur on Amina started to peel off in the rain. After the fur fell at her feet, Amina did not waste any time, she ran as fast as she could, towards her house. When she got home, her mother was so relieved she had returned that she forgot how angry she was before. She made Amina some hot dinner, after Amina had taken a hot bath.

On the other side of town, Rabbit Girl, now a human girl, had been sitting on a bench, eating some hot rice and stew she had been offered by a kind family. Their little boy screamed, suddenly, when the girl at the table, started to shrink and develop rabbit features. The Rabbit found itself on the floor of the table, and then hopped out of the house, towards the forest. The family looked at each other in amazement. Neither of them uttered a word to each other about what they had just seen.

Amina never returned to that side of the forest where she had met the rabbit, also formerly known as rabbit girl. She never told anyone of her experiences with Rabbit Girl. Who would have believed her anyway?

The Winding Staircase

Their car stopped suddenly, in front of a crumbling, old mansion. Her parents had always had a love for old houses. They hardly stayed in one town for more than a year. Amelia's parents were very adventurous, and loved to travel. They moved from one place to another in search of new adventures, and a new and simple way of life. They had always found work in the neighbouring towns and did not mind what they did. In one town, her mother had worked as a florist in a shop, whilst her father had found work in a bakery. Both parents had been doctors in the big city; but one day, they decided they had made enough money and wanted to travel the world.

Amelia was a quiet child. At the young age of five, she had been plucked (and that's how she came to see it at the age of twelve) from the life she had ever known, since she could remember anything, to travel the world. She had never liked any of the towns they had moved to. She felt her parents were never considerate in their decision to become nomads. She was always attending into different schools and each time, she had to adjust to the environment, try to make new friends and fit into her new community. Unfortunately, she felt she had never fitted anywhere they went to. Amelia missed the noise of the city: the police car sirens, the voice of the woman below her bedroom window shouting across the road to anyone interested in buying her flowers and the excited barking of the dogs being taken out for their daily walk.

So, as they all stood in front of this old crumbling mansion, with paint peeling off the walls, she wondered whether this crumbling mansion would become the home she had always longed for. She wanted to belong somewhere. She just wished her parents would settle down at one place and get proper jobs. In a month, in the previous town, her father had worked a builder, a postman and a family doctor. What did he want to do with his life, she often wondered? Her parents were both 40 years old. Too old, she thought, to be so indecisive about what they wanted in life.

'Darling, do you like our new house?' Her mother asked, pulling her towards the front door whilst her father struggled to carry two suitcases behind them. Amelia glanced at her mother and saw how excited she was. Amelia smiled thinly at her mother, in answer to the question and allowed her mother to lead her through the house. Even though the house was crumbling on the outside the interior of the house had been newly decorated. There was a staircase from the sitting room leading to the second floor where the bedrooms were.

Amelia's mother pulled her hand excitedly and opened her door to new bedroom. Her parents had decided for the rooms to be refurbished before they moved in. Looking around the room, Amelia noticed that her wallpaper was green. At least, her mother had listened to her suggestion of having a different colour to pink. Her bed covers were green and felt fresh to the touch. There were framed pictures of some plants Amelia had drawn.

'Thanks mom'. Amelia smiled quietly.

'Do you like it, darling?' Her mother asked.

'Yes'.

Her mother left the room, closing the door quietly behind her. Amelia could hear her running down the stairs in excitement.

Amelia threw herself onto the bed and lay face up, staring at the ceiling. She was starting her new school the next day. Another new school! She was so exhausted of all these changes. She closed her eyes and prayed silently that her parents would love this town.

Amelia woke up with a start!

She could hear her mother calling out to her.

'Dinnertime!'

It seemed she had fallen asleep for about 45 minutes. Her eyes followed the long hands of the clock as it went tick tocking all around the clock. Amelia pushed herself up and walked down the stairs for dinner.

'Come on dear'. Her father said. 'We have just moved into a nice new house. At the dinner table, as her father cut his meat, a little too vigorously with his knife, he said 'You should be excited! This may be our final stop!' He stuffed some vegetables and potato onto a fork, and then looked at his daughter with concern, as she had not said a word and was swirling her food around her plate. Obviously, all the moving around was taking a toll on their only daughter.

Amelia saw the concern on her parents faces as they ate their dinner whilst talking to her. She made a mental note to try to love the new house, her new school and town.

'Goodnight'. She said, after she had finished her food and skipped upstairs to her room.

She wanted to appear happy, but she was not. She missed the city and her friends. She was tired of moving. In her room, she fell asleep whilst reading her new book: The House of Horrors. She half smiled when she fell asleep. She had imagined her new house as a house of horrors.

'At least, that would be something to look forward to . . .' She muttered to herself and fell asleep shortly.

Amelia woke up with a start. She looked around her quickly, remembering as she did so that she was in a new house in the country, located somewhere. Her clock said it was 15 minutes after midnight. She got out of bed and looked out of her window. The trees were swaying gently as the wind outside wheezed through them. The sky was clear and quite bright with so many stars shining. She stood looking out of the window for a while, wondering what this new place had in store for her. What would her new school be like? Would she like it? She had never made any friends at any of the other schools she had attended after the one in the city. She had not wanted to make and later break friendships. Unfortunately, that meant she was alone most of the time.

Amelia heard a slight noise again. This time, it sounded like it was coming from outside her bedroom. As she walked towards the door, she caught sight of her book: the house of horrors, lying upside down on her bed. A shudder went through her as she briefly imagined that her new house was indeed the house of horrors. She reached the door and opened it to a crack at first.

She could not see anything outside her door because the corridor light had been put off for the night. She could not remember where the switch was, however, she relied on the moonlight coming through her bedroom window. She stepped out of her bedroom, walked to the end of the corridor and, came up to a door she had not seen before. She stood in front of it for a full minute wondering whether she should open it or go back to bed. She rested her hand on the handle and looked behind her towards her parents' bedroom, which was opposite her bedroom. There was no sound. The atmosphere in the house was still and silent.

Amelia inhaled shakily and turned the door handle. The door creaked and swung open. As she went through the door, she saw a winding staircase, like the one in the large hall downstairs, leading up to what seemed to be an attic. Upon reaching the top of the staircase, Amelia pushed the attic door open.

As soon as Amelia stepped into the attic, the whole room lit up and there was what sounded like dreamy music coming from an old radio on the table. She stood still and surveyed her surroundings. She contemplated going back to her room but there was something about the music being played. The music was soft and beckoning in a way. Amelia walked towards the radio and turned the music up slightly. Suddenly, all around her, gold dust appeared, and the room started to spin. She fell onto her knees with her hands covering her face. And then, just as suddenly as the spinning had started, it stopped. Her eyes had been closed all this while. She felt tired suddenly and wanted to continue lying down on the floor.

Only it wasn't a floor, it was a bed!!

Amelia sat up.

Where am I? She screamed in her head. She tried to talk but her throat hurt. Then suddenly, the bedroom door opened.

'Princess Amelia! Are you still sleeping? Your mother, the Queen, would like to see you downstairs. You did not come down for breakfast this morning'. The maid said.

Amelia raised her head slowly. She felt a little dizzy. She looked at the maid, all dressed up in a white starched uniform and a matching white hat. She blinked a few times. Then she looked around her. It seemed she was in a castle. Her bedroom was furnished in pink and purple. On the table in front of a large mirror, was a crown.

As the maid helped Amelia out of bed, it dawned on her that she was a Princess in this strange castle. She went to the bathroom and brushed her teeth, brushed her hair and wore her clothes, which had been laid out on the bed whilst she was in the bathroom. The maid was still waiting for her near the door.

Amelia placed the crown carefully on her head and followed the maid downstairs, in anticipation of what awaited her there. Amelia was worried about how she would get back to the attic and therefore back to her room. She decided to go back into the room as soon as she had met with the Queen and find a way back.

'Ah, Amelia'. The Queen said with a smile, when she saw Amelia walking towards her. She had been knitting something that looked like a small woollen hat to Amelia.

'Sit beside me, my dear. Have you thought about what we last spoke about?' The Queen said, looking at Amelia expectantly.

Amelia gave a small cough, trying to play for time in order to figure out what it was that she and her mother, the Queen, had talked about. How could she be in one world at a one time and in another world, the next?

'I don't . . .' She started to say.

Her mother gave impatient snot.

'It's your birthday tomorrow as you are aware, you will be thirteen years old. We are having young people, your age, from other royal families over here in the palace for a picnic. Do you want to have a maze and other games set up in the garden grounds or do you want a singing and dancing competition?'

Amelia shifted uncomfortably in her seat. She was a bit of an introvert. She liked keeping to herself most of the time, reading a good book and just getting on with things she could do herself. How was it that over here, she was having a party for her birthday? She had never had a birthday party. Her parents had suggested it, but she had always refused and they had never pressed her to have it.

'. . . really must decide now so we know what we are doing for you tomorrow'. The Queen continued.

'I will have a maze and other games set up, mother'. Amelia said.

'Great! Have some breakfast and go out into the garden. The workers are already setting up the maze. I knew you would choose that'. The Queen said with a smile.

Amelia walked towards the garden and saw workers hammering everywhere and setting games- she had no idea what they were. She felt tired and walked back up to her bedroom. In the bedroom, she looked for a trapdoor that would lead her back into the attic, down the winding stairs and back into her bedroom. She could not see or make out a trapdoor of any kind. She felt tired and decided to sleep for a bit.

The next morning arrived. Amelia was woken up by one of her attendants. She looked around her worriedly. She could not believe she was still here; in this strange kingdom where she was a princess. She was directed to a bathtub and was made to take a bath and then dressed up in a long yellow and white dress with a matching golden tiara. Her parents, the King and Queen were waiting for her in the throne room.

'Happy Birthday, dear', her mother said, smiling broadly. Her father came towards her and clasped both her hands in his.

'Happy Birthday, Amelia', He said sullenly. He was a man of very few words, but was considered a great king by many.

'Come Amelia, let's go to the garden where everything has been laid out for your party.

The party turned out to be Amelia's most exciting experience in her lifetime.

She spent a lot of time with the other children and young people who had attended. There was music all day long, and so much food to eat. She and other young people run through the maze chasing after each other. Amelia got lost several times, but someone always found her. After a while, Amelia felt tired, and decided to take a nap. She looked around the garden for a corner or anywhere she could lay her head for a few minutes.

She saw a tree house in the corner of the garden where a dog resting at the bottom of the treehouse. Amelia used the steps on the trunk of the main tree and pulled at the branch leading into the treehouse. When she stepped in, she found two large cushions on the floor and some toys, which meant some children had been in there earlier and had played some games using these toys. Amelia pushed the toys away and made enough room for her to lie down for a few minutes. Amelia slept right away as she was so tired from all the day's activities.

'Amelia! Amelia . . .!' Amelia could hear her name being called. The sound seemed to be coming from a distance away. She woke up suddenly, looking around her frantically. She had to go back to the party before her parents, the King and Queen, noticed she had gone missing from her party.

'Wait . . .' Amelia mumbled to herself. 'I am back home . . .'. Amelia's mother burst into her room.

'Amelia! You were not in your room . . .and what are you doing up here in the attic. You must have overslept! Anyway, hurry up and get dressed. We must take you to school, and you cannot be late, as this is your first day of school.

'Ok Mom. I am sorry, I was just exploring the house. I will be down soon'.

Amelia waited for her mother to leave the attic. As she turned her head, slowly, towards the trapdoor, in the corner of the room, a green light shifted beneath the floorboard. Amelia knew that if she opened the trapdoor, she will be back in that world: a world of magic and make-belief; away from her reality of being in this new town and going to a new school.

Amelia stood for a few minutes lost in thought. She turned towards the door, that would lead her out of the attic, and back to her bedroom. Amelia took a few steps towards the door, and then without a moment's hesitation, she turned swiftly and headed towards the trapdoor, towards the world of magic and make-belief.

The Mysterious Beautiful Woman

In a small town, far away from other towns, in a certain country, there were houses, lined up on streets with beautiful gardens in front of the houses. Everything was perfect in this town. The streets were clean and tidy. Rubbish bins lined up on the street so that no one threw anything on the ground. The air smelt clean and fresh. Everything was perfect, until a woman moved into one of the houses on the street. No one knew where she had come from. Everyone woke up one morning to discover that there was a new resident living in a house that had been vacant for many years. There were sweet smells of baked cakes, pies and warm bread coming out of her window.

Also, the garden in front of her house, suddenly, had roses of every colour growing in it. There were red, yellow, white, pink and even green roses growing in the garden and their smell was just glorious. This was quite strange, as all her neighbours knew that garden had been overgrown with weeds just the evening before. Before long, people started gathering in front of the woman's house, hoping to catch a glimpse of her. People were arguing amongst themselves. Some said they did not remember there being any roses in the garden and others said it was impossible for roses to grow over night and that they must have been growing all along without anyone noticing. However, because they could not fathom how it was that there were now flowers growing in the garden, they dismissed these thoughts and went about with their daily lives.

Meanwhile, the woman had opened her curtain a little bit and was watching the growing crowds gathering in front of her house. A smile formed on her lips, as she thought of all the plans she had in store for her neighbours. She waited for another five minutes and then went out carrying a tray of small cakes for everyone to taste. The people could not stop themselves from taking a bite of the cakes. After they talked about the town for a while, the woman went back into the house, and everyone went about their business.

The woman was about thirty years old and was very beautiful with long black hair and violet eyes. However, she had a secret. She was not as young as she looked. She was a hundred and three years old. Her secret was that to keep looking forever young, she must bake cakes and feed them to her neighbours in whatever town she lived in. She would then use the crumbs of the leftover cakes and bread and scatter them over her rose garden. She had to keep moving from town to town whenever her secret was discovered. She hoped that she would be able to stay a bit longer in this town.

To her, the people seemed innocent and friendly. She shuddered to think of what had happened when her secret had been discovered in the last town she had lived in. Her secret had been discovered when a little boy had innocently found the crumbs in a corner of her house, during a party, and eaten them. She had aged instantly in front of the guests she was entertaining in her living room. This was because the little boy had eaten the ingredients to her becoming young. Everyone had screamed and watched as she became old in front of their very eyes. Her hair had become white, and her bones had appeared to stick out of her skin. Of course, when they had left, she had collected all the crumbs from their plates, made the secret potion and drank it.

After her youthful appearance returned, she had left the town in the middle of the night. Thinking back to that day, she frowned and shook her head quickly to forget that awful memory. And so it was that every day, the people of her new town were invited to the woman's house to eat her baked goodies. They danced to music and were very merry.

The people of this town welcomed the new activities due to the newcomer's arrival. Here was a woman who did not have a family like everyone else, had a lovely garden with beautiful rose bushes they had never seen before and seemed not to have a care in the world. There however a young man of about eighteen years old who hoped that the woman would pay him some attention and marry him someday even though she was years older than him. One day, when all the neighbours came to the woman's house as usual for her tea parties, as she liked to call them. He noticed how carefully she collected the crumbs off the neighbours' plates and poured them into transparent bags. After that she pulled a vanity case from behind one of the sofas and carefully put the bag into this. This went on for weeks. He began to wonder what she did with them. One evening, he could not sleep so he quietly opened the front door of his parents' house and walked out. He found himself walking towards the house of the mystery woman.

As he drew nearer, he saw her sprinkling something that looked like crumbs on to the rose bushes. To his amazement, some of them start shooting more rosebuds in front of his eyes. He rubbed his eyes and slapped his cheeks. I must be dreaming, he said to himself. But when he took his hands off his face, he could still see more roses flowering. He hid quickly behind a large oak tree that had a thick trunk and wide branches. The woman then plucked the freshest roses and hurried back into the house. By then, the young man could see that her face was distorted. It was no longer young but had become very old with hundreds of wrinkles.

The young man was so shocked he almost fell from behind the tree. But he had to keep on watching, he said to himself. Luckily for him, the kitchen she had entered was facing the roadside and he could see everything. She had forgotten to draw the curtains in her haste. She seemed to be mixing a potion, and then she applied the mixture to her face. In the meantime, in the woman's house, she was cursing herself for having forgotten to set her alarm to make the potion. She had just woken up by chance.

Now she had to rush to get this portion on her face before she withered and shrank to nothing. Just before she closed the curtain, she thought she saw that young man who lived across the road peeping from behind a tree. 'How much does he know?' she wondered. She had seen him staring at her, too closely for her liking over the past few weeks. Unknown to her, the young man had seen everything but did not know what to do with this information. He decided to wait for a few days before he told anyone about what he had seen. What people did not realise was, the more the woman used the leftover crumbs of her neighbours in her potion mixture, the harder it was for the crops in their farms and back gardens to flourish. She was taking away their prosperity. The woman must be stopped from using their crumbs or leftovers to make herself beautiful. He still could not believe it. The next day, the young man went about his business as usual. He decided not to tell anyone about his discovery until he had made up his mind about what to do. When he went back home after his day's work, he saw an invitation on his parents' table.

There was to be a big party at the mysterious woman's house, and all were invited. Everyone was to come well dressed. The young man realised that the woman was probably thinking about leaving town because he suspected she had seen him looking at her. He felt this strongly. He had a plan. There was loud music booming from the house. The long table which had been pushed to a corner of the large sitting room was laden with all kinds of meats, sweets, and cakes. There were cold drinks in big buckets of ice. Everything was going smoothly or so the woman thought.

When the young man thought the woman was not looking, he sneaked upstairs into the woman's room. He was looking for the special wooden spoon she used to mix the crumbs as well as the liquid in a small bottle she poured over the crumbs before eating them together with the fresh roses she collected from the garden. After a quick search, he discovered the items wrapped up in cloth. He looked around the room and just as he had suspected the beautiful mysterious woman was planning to leave town soon. Everything was packed up.

The young man quickly slipped out of the room with the wooden spoon and liquid and took them to his house. He poured the contents of the bottle away and filled the bottle with a liquid that looked like the one that was in it. He had a spoon just like the woman's spoon. He looked across the street and from his window he could see that the party was still going on. He went back to the woman's house and put the items in her room quickly. The party went on until about ten o'clock in the evening. When everyone went home, the woman sang along as she gathered the crumbs of the left-over cakes and pastries. She looked at the clock and realized she had only thirty minutes to start preparing her mixture. She went upstairs and took out the bottle with the special liquid as well as her wooden spoon. She went downstairs to the kitchen and poured all the crumbs into a wooden bowl. Then she poured the liquid over the crumbs. The mixture should have started turning pale blue. After twenty minutes, nothing happened. She started to panic and started screaming and crying.

In the meantime, the noise coming from her house had attracted many people who had been disturbed from their sleep. People were gathered outside her house wondering what action to take. Should they go in or should they wait for a while? Then the young man from across the street pushed through the crowd and raised his voice and quickly explained what he had noticed about the woman, and how she used left over crumbs to make herself look beautiful and how he had replaced her items for fake ones. Some people believed him, and others did not. Then a few men forced themselves into the house and were surprised to see a very old woman on the floor. Her skin was getting wrinkled very quickly and her body was shrinking rapidly. The young man saw this and was shocked even though he had seen this before. He was very sorry that he had taken the items.

He quickly run over to his house and brought the real items, looked around for more crumbs and quickly mixed and gently made the woman drink the concoction. All who had gathered around, were very surprised to see the woman transform from an old woman, back to the beautiful woman she had been before. The villagers after overcoming their shock forced the woman to pack all her belongings and leave town immediately. It was considered bad luck for someone to secretly collect the crumbs off another's plate. In other words, the woman had been 'stealing' their good luck. The next day, life went on as usual, people went to work. Others went into their garden and started planting rose bushes. They had cut some rose stems from the woman's garden. Life went on as usual After a few weeks, everyone had forgotten about the mysterious young woman.

One evening when most people were sitting on their porches or verandas listening to music and talking softly amongst themselves, a large van pulled up in front of the house the mysterious beautiful woman used to live. It was still the only unoccupied house in the neighbourhood. The movers brought out all the items from the van and took them into the house. People were craning their necks from their balconies, as they could not see who was moving into the house. Just when most of them had given up hope of ever seeing anyone walk towards the house, out stepped a short dwarf-like man with a long beard and a bushy moustache. When the side door of the van opened, out stepped a beautiful young woman. She was wearing a huge wedding ring on her finger. The woman turned towards the neighbours and waved. A few waved back. Unbeknownst to any of them, the beautiful woman was the same one who used to live there a few months ago and she had more plans for her neighbours. With a small smile, she went followed her husband into her house. 'Oh yes', she thought to herself, 'I have so much in store for you. I will take my revenge out on you for disgracing and chasing me out of this town'.

The young man from across the street whispered to himself. 'What is it with this house?' And with that he walked into his house and went about his duties.

All That Glitters

There is a famous saying that 'all that glitters is not gold'. In this story we are going to see how true this famous saying is. In the kingdom of Zayon, there lived many families in linear cottages. The arrangement of the cottages was such that one could most often see what went on in the other cottage, if the windows or curtains were open. In house number three and number four, there lived two families who lived in cottages that were opposite each other. The Brown family were very rich and had two children aged five and seven, a boy and a girl, respectively.

Mrs Brown was aware that she and her husband were very rich. They had a vineyard and made the best wines in the kingdom. They could therefore afford anything they wanted. The whole family wore very fine clothes, and they had the respect of everyone in the area. On the other hand, the Tray family had just enough money. They were comfortable. Their cottage was large enough for them. They had girl triplets aged four. They had a garden as well, though not as large as the Browns. Mrs Brown and Mrs Tray were friends despite the difference in their fortunes. Mrs Brown was about 5'4" and a bit chubby with a pretty face. She had shoulder length hair and loved to dress up a great deal even when she was only going to Mrs Tray's house for a visit. Mrs Tray on the other hand, was a tall woman and had very long hair up to her waist which she liked to put in a single braid most of the time. So it was that even though both women were as different as chalk and cheese, they were good friends.

One of the things they talked about most of the time, was how they would like to experience the life of the other if only for a day. Mrs Tray envied the life of Mrs Brown because she could only see what was on the surface- the riches and glamorous lifestyle, the cooks, and maidservants. Mrs Brown was not helping the situation at all by boasting about everything her husband bought for her and the children. One day, a gypsy woman selling her wares was passing by when she heard Mrs Brown telling her Mrs Tray; '… so he is planning on taking me and the children to Greenland, and he will be buying us …' and she went on to describe all the things her husband was going to buy for her.

Now Greenland in those days was the equivalent of what Paris, Rome and London are today. With a smile on the gypsy woman's face, she took out some gold dust and sprinkled it in the air. The gold dust as if it were alive made its way to where the ladies were sitting and settled on them. Immediately, both women started spinning and before they realised, they had swapped bodies, so Mrs Tray became Mrs Brown and Mrs Brown became Mrs Tray. When they realised what had happened, they cried and screamed but they could not do anything about it.

So, Mrs Brown had to go to Mrs Tray's house and Mrs Tray had to go to Mrs Brown's house. They agreed to meet the following morning after the children had gone to school and their 'husbands' had gone to work. In a way, Mrs Tray was happy she was going to see how life was in the Brown's house. She had to pretend to be Mrs Brown.

She played with the children and put them to bed. While waiting for Mr Brown to return from work, she walked round the house starting from the kitchen where there were neatly arranged cooking bowls, China plates and cups. She made her way through the living room where she admired all the gold and silver decorations, and she ended up in the bedroom. She was surprised that there were two separate bedrooms for both Mr and Mrs Brown. She went into Mrs Brown's walk-in closet and was so surprised by the number of gold, silver and pearl necklaces that were flowing out of jewellery pots. These were on the table in front of the dressing mirror. She peered into the wardrobe and opened her mouth in amazement: so many clothes of all colours. She was so happy she forgot about how much she missed her husband and children. She took her bath in the fake ivory bath basin and chose a light green long evening dress with matching earrings and waited for Mr Brown in the front porch of the house. When his carriage arrived, she stood up and smiled and said 'hello' with a very bright smile.

Mr Brown was thinking to himself 'mmm, something must be different today because usually on a night like this …' and with this thought he looked at the sky. After they had their meal talking about this and that, they retired to their separate bedrooms. Now, Mrs Tray was going to discover why they slept in different bedrooms. The sky was very bright outside and there was a full moon.

Now, across the street, Mrs Brown had to become Mrs Tray in her friend's house that evening. Her friend's house was smaller than her spacious cottage. It was neat and cute, she thought to herself. The children ran to her and luckily for her, all she had to do was warm some food that had already been prepared by their mother, for them to have as supper. She asked them what they wanted to do the next day. While they were talking, she was wondering what her friend would think about her after what she would see tonight. She went into her friend's room. At least, she shares a room with her husband, she thought to herself. In the middle of her thoughts, her friend's husband came back from work and the whole family played snakes and ladders for an hour and then went to bed. That night, Mrs Brown told her husband that she wanted to go for a walk because she was not feeling too well. Mr Tray thought his wife was behaving a bit strangely but then thought to himself that women were a little complex anyway and left it at that. Shortly, he went to bed because he had to wake up early to go to his carpentry shop. As the real Mrs Brown walked outside on a long walk, she looked anxious towards her family's house and then looked up. The sky was a clear blue, she noticed and there was a full moon. She walked for a while and went back into the house.

On a night like this when there were clear skies and a full moon, Mrs Tray would go to bed early so as not to witness what happened to him. But today, she had come to meet him at the door. He brushed this thought aside and went to his bedroom to get ready for what was about to happen. In the middle of the night, Mrs Tray was asleep in the bedroom next to his. She was really enjoying lying on the silk bed sheets as compared to her cotton ones. She was smiling to herself when she heard a strange noise coming from the next room. They were animal -like sounds. Wanting to satisfy her curiosity, she opened Mr Brown's room slightly. What met her eyes was to remain with her for the rest of her life. She watched Mr Brown become a beast and afterwards, he sat down on the chair in front of his dressing mirror, combed his fur and then removed the hairs from the brush, and placed this in a glass jar.

Mrs Tray had heard all kinds of stories about how people became rich by doing all sorts of things. As she had correctly suspected, this was how the Browns made their money. Their vineyard had juicy grapes even during the dry season when there was no rain. Mrs Tray went to the bathroom where she became quite ill. After a while, she went to bed wondering how on earth she was going to tell her husband that she and her friends had swapped bodies. The next morning when she woke up, Mr Brown had already left for work. She realised that this family was not as close as hers. He hardly spoke to his wife and the children were looked after by the servants. They seemed to be happy, but they were not. She realised that riches were not everything. Happiness was the most important thing. She started to cry quietly to herself.

In the meantime, Mrs Brown on the other hand, had woken up and was wondering about how she was going to feed the whole household when she thought she saw some gold dust coming towards her through the window. At the same time, the gold dust was making its way to Mrs Tray who was still in Mrs Brown's house crying. Within minutes, the gold dust had worked its magic and both women were not only in their own bodies but found themselves with their families in their own house.

Shaking with relief, both were happy for different reasons. Mrs Brown knew that even though monsters visited her husband every full moon, at least she did not have to cook, clean and look after her children. Mrs Tray was glad that despite not being rich, she and her husband were happy and did not have to 'look forward' to her husband transforming on every full moon. Both women remained friends but never spoke about what had happened that night, not to anyone, not even to themselves. They pretended it never happened. They both felt happy with their lives and did not speak of wanting to be the other, ever again.

However, Mrs Tray now realised that 'all that glitters is not gold'.

The Boarding School of Mysteries

Jamie waved to his parents as they pulled away from the school car park. He looked down at his two suitcases and wondered how he was going to carry them to his room after the house master who was standing a few steps away from him, allocated his room to him. As he looked around the car park, he could see several 15-year-old boys like him being dropped off by their parents. Some looked sad; others looked happy to finally break away from their parents and stay in the boarding house of St. Peter's College. The college had re-opened for the new term a week earlier for the 2nd and 3rd year students. The 1st year students were all told to arrive today- Sunday afternoon by 5pm, for their first year in the college. This was a college for Science and Technology and one of the best in the country.

Jamie stood near the offices at the edge of the car park and waited for the housemaster to give him the key to his room. He had heard from friends that three first year students shared a room. There was supposed to be a bunk bed and a single bed. He wondered who was going to get the single bed as that was preferred by most students. He also had the experience of falling off a bunk bed in his previous boarding school. So, the thought of sleeping on the top bed put him off. His thoughts were interrupted by two boys of his age coming towards him. They had also been dropped off by their parents and said the house master wanted to see him.

'Hey there. I am Michael and that is Brian. We are cousins'.

Michael smiled and held out his hand to Jamie. 'Hi. It is nice to meet you. Are you in first year too?' Jamie replied after a firm handshake. He guessed correctly that Michael was trying to 'out-shake' him. 'Well, the house master wants to see us to give us our room number so let's go'. The three boys walked towards the house master. They felt very at ease with each other as they talked about similar interests such as basketball, football and tennis. The boys settled into their room.

Michael ended up on the single bed as they tossed a coin for it, and he won. Jamie was on the lower bunk bed and Brian was on the top bunk bed. They each had a small wardrobe and after they had arranged their clothes and pictures on the dressing table which they had to share. Their room was so comfortable that the boys felt that they were 'home away from home'. Their door was green in colour and the only green door on a corridor of 12 doors. The house master had said to them; '… and here is your key. It is for the green door on the ground floor of the junior dormitory'.

The boys had found trolleys for their suitcases and were so intent on pushing them to their room that no one had looked at the door number. It was when they were on their way to the dining hall for their 6pm dinner that they all said together: 'Number 13!'

Just like in the American movies they had watched, the boys believed that the number 13 was an unlucky number. It was however too late for any room changes to be done as every student who wanted to start the first-year course in Science and Technology, had arrived and taken up all the rooms. They went to the dining hall. Each one absorbed in their thoughts. Dinner was egg fried rice with fish and chicken. It was not as nice as what the boys were used to at home but at least, it filled their stomachs for the night.

The first week at college was very busy. The program for the students was filled with course inductions, introduction to teachers and introductory lessons. The boys made friends with their other classmates, but they were still good friends, and this made getting along easier especially as they were roommates. Everything was going fi ne. Lessons were good and they had settled. They were however kind of waiting for something exciting to happen. There were a few films showed in the great hall. Apart from these, Brian, Jamie and Michael, being boys of adventurous expectations, were quite bored. They enjoyed some of their lessons, some of the time, but found college a bit boring and monotonous, most of the time.

However, this was all to change in their fourth week. The boys were taking a walk around the campus. The campus land was very extensive. There were also some farms adjoining the campus that belonged to the local farmers. They were walking leisurely on the borders of some farms, when a farmer came out of nowhere and said to them; 'Are you from that college there yonder? he pointed towards their college. 'Yes, we are', Jamie said.

'Well,' the man said, with some hesitation, 'I must tell you, the land upon which the college was built used to be a cemetery. It is haunted at night by different ghosts.

The three most popular ones are Lady High Heels, the Flying Tree and the dancing queens'. He said with a worried look on his face.

'What has that got to do with us?' Brian retorted.

'Oh, you will see... considering that you are in Room 13. Hahaha', he laughed and disappeared into thin air.

The boys screamed and started running towards their dormitory drawing curious looks from the other students around. That night was to be the beginning of their experiences. Everyone was asleep in the dormitory.

Brian, Jamie and Michael had only just fallen asleep after telling each other stories about their families, brothers and sisters. It was Jamie who heard the actual sound of heels 'clacking' on the roof. 'Clack, clack,

clack'. To him, it sounded like someone wearing very high heels walking up and down the roof. Without waking the others up, he went outside and looked on the rooftop. He could hear the sound of high heels but did not see anyone. He saw a student who was coming back from late night studies going to one of the rooms on the corridor. He beckoned for him to come. 'Say, can you hear the sound of heels on the roof?'

'No'. The other student said with a look of amazement on his face. Everyone knew that Brian, Michael and Jamie were always up to some mischief when they were not studying, so he thought it was one of their pranks. He shook his head and walked away. Jamie could still hear someone with high heels going up and down the roof. Unknown to Jamie, he and his friends Michael and Brian were the only ones who would hear and see all the strange happenings. This was because they were in room number 13.

Jamie went back to the room and woke the other boys up. He quickly told them what he had heard. They strained their ears and discovered that they too could hear heels going up and down their roof. There was a drainage pipe connected from the chimney on the roof top to the ground. They decided to climb up the drainage pipe and get to the roof top. What met their eyes took their breath away. There, on the roof top, was the so called 'Lady High Heels. She was all dressed up in a pink prom-like dress with very high pink heels. Her hair was shining and of a silver colour. Her lips were full and a bright pink.

If the boys had not reminded themselves that they were on the roof top of their dormitory, they would have thought they were witnessing a fashion show. Only, it seemed the woman was from the old ages: the period of fairies and Cinderella. The lady of about 20 years of age, seemed to be walking up and down, looking from left to right, bowing and curtsying every so often as if there was a grand audience watching her. The boys were very surprised. They could not say a word. Then Michael went up to her and tried to touch her, but of course she was a ghost, so his hand went through her. Then she started crying and saying: 'He does not want to dance with me. Where is he? He said he would be here'. So it was, that she continued walking up and down the roof top, searching through the imaginary crowds, as if looking for someone. The boys observed that she kept stopping every so often, and would put her face in her hands, crying, whilst repeatedly saying, 'he does not want to dance with me'. After walking up and down the roof for an hour she screamed and disappeared.

The boys hurried down from the roof and decided to talk about this in the morning as they had to go to sleep quickly to wake up in time for their morning lesson.

The following day went by in a blur as all the boys wanted was for night to fall so that they could talk about what they had seen the previous night and if possible, see the Lady High Heels again. They had agreed amongst themselves that it was no use telling anyone about what they had seen because no one would believe them.

In the evening, they went for their evening studies in the classroom as usual. During this period, everyone read their notes quietly and there was a teacher who supervised these studies to make sure that everyone was studying. It was only after these studies that Brian, Michael and Jamie talked about what they would do that evening. Despite the fact that the boys were a bit afraid and shocked about what they had seen, they were still very curious about the fact that the college was built on an old cemetery ground.

It was about 10 pm and everyone was in their rooms, talking and reading and eating their snacks. The boys quickly had some juice and biscuits and decided to go for a walk using a footpath behind the dormitory. They walked very fast because they wanted to go into the middle of the forest. The whole campus was built in the middle of a forest and there were trees everywhere. When they reached the centre of the forest, they realised that there was a clearing. In the middle of the forest, stood one very large tree. It was a tall tree, with a thick trunk and many branches. At the topmost part of the tree was a white owl with big bright eyes.

The boys were very taken aback with the beauty of the owl and before they could say anything the tree tore itself from the ground and flew a few feet off the ground and planted itself back into the soil but not in the same spot so that the boys could see a deep hole from where the tree originally was. They started walking slowly away from the scene and then started running. They reached their door after 10 minutes with all three boys trying to squeeze past the door at the same time.

'Whew!' said Jamie.

'What was that?' Michael asked, short of breath.

'I think we have to tell someone', suggested Brian.

After that incident, for a month, the boys saw nothing out of the ordinary. They were beginning to enjoy life at college. They went to a few dances organised with the girls' college which was a few miles from their college. It was at one of these dances that the boys had another ghostly experience. The excitement in the boys' dormitory was very high.

First of all, the fact that the annual dance was at a girls' college was a plus, because they were going to see and make friends with girls and then the mere fact that they were leaving the college campus for the evening, was also a reason for this excitement. A coach had been arranged for the boys' transfer to the girls' college. While on the coach, they sang several songs and danced along the aisle in excitement. The housemaster had a lot of trouble keeping the boys calm.

Soon, they arrived at the dance. The girls were just as glad to see boys in their college as they were hardly out of the college themselves. The dance had been set up in what was known as the 'great hall'. The Great Hall had been a site for ceremonies like speech and prize giving day, graduations, and the daily morning assembly. On a special night like this, the hall was decorated with balloons of all colours. The banners of both colleges were on each side of the wall and there were a few chairs arranged on a stage for the teachers to supervise students but apart from that, the central part of the hall was bare- mainly because of the dancing that was to take place. Boys stood on one side and girls stood on the other.

Michael, Jamie and Brian were eagerly awaiting the start of the dance so they could choose their dance partners. All the boys were dressed in white shirts, and black trousers and the girls were dressed on white blouses and long black skirts. It was a beautiful event. Soon, the dancing began and the boys were allowed to choose their partners. Brian, Michael, and Jamie were just about to give up hope of getting partners when three girls rushed towards them and started swirling them around the dance floor. The boys were pleasantly surprised and happy to have found such good dance partners. Suddenly, they heard some strange music. It sounded very eerie and at the same time, it sounded very sweet.

In the meantime, they looked over at the other dancers and it seemed they were the only ones who could hear that kind of music. Before they realised, they were out of the dance hall with the strange girls and still dancing but this time, they were moving towards a dark part of the school. No one saw them, even though Jamie tried to scream. The faces of the girls started to change. They looked like old witches. Their clothes were torn. The boys began to scream, and they tried to break free from these dancing witches.

It was the second day of college for the boys. Brian, Jamie and Michael, had all had a series of very disturbing sleeps and many awful dreams. The boys looked at each other and each one of them had a look of surprise. They asked each other in turn, about the 'flying tree', 'the lady high heels' and 'the dancing queens'. They all nodded.

How could they all have had the same dreams? Something strange was going on.

After breakfast at the dining hall, they went to the headmaster's house and told him they wanted a room change, but they could not tell him the reason why.

To their surprise, the headmaster gave them a key to room number '31'. As they headed to their new room, he turned with a twinkle in his eye and gave them a wink. 'Better luck this time'. He closed the door to his house and roared with laughter.

Little did the boys know what was waiting for them in that room. As they entered the room, they all fell through a trap door. 'Oh no!

What next?' Jamie screamed.

So, the question is, were their experiences real or were they just dreams?

The Night Before Halloween

After what I had witnessed the night before, it was no surprise that I froze in shock when whilst walking to work, I saw the very same Halloween pumpkin, on the doorstep of my neighbour's house. I could not move. My hand moved quickly to my throat, where I clutched my imaginary pearls. This could not be, I thought to myself.

So, it all began yesterday – the evening of Halloween.

The streets had echoed from one end to the other, with the excited voices of children running up and down the street: moving from one door to the next in their quest of 'Trick or Treating'. The smaller children were being supervised by their parents, and were also dressed in funny costumes, though not as scary as those worn by their children.

I had stood at my bathroom window and had marvelled at the various Halloween decorations that adorned the front porches of my neighbours' houses. The decorations ranged from stringed glowing lights, floating ghosts that made loud screams when someone came too close; large, decorated pumpkins with glowing eyes and jaggered teeth carved into them to mahogany and silver hanging bats.

My house was the odd one on the street. It was as plain as the word itself.

Earlier in the day, when I was going to work, some eyes darted towards me as I walked past as if to say; 'do you not know what day it is', but I had no intention of celebrating Halloween. I was the odd one out, but I did not mind. I was a quiet 30-year-old woman, with no pets or friends. I had moved into this neighbourhood to start a new life. I was friendly with my neighbours, and they were polite in their conversations with me. But that was that. I do not have to celebrate Halloween or any other festivities with them.

On this evening, as Halloween progressed, I moved away from the bathroom window, where I had been watching the activities on the street. I went to the kitchen to get a glass of wine, and my dinner. I ate my dinner and watched some TV programmes, with the sounds of the festivities and children's excited screams coming through my window.

I must have fallen asleep, because when I woke up, the house was in darkness. The Television had those lines running across when the channel had been shut for the night. Why was the house in darkness? I had had the lights on. The atmosphere in the house felt very eerie.

I had lived by myself for eight years, since I left home. I had never felt as petrified as I felt now. Was it my imagination, or had the air in the room suddenly turned cold? I was still sitting on the couch, unable to move or get up. My plate and wine glass were still on the side table next to me. My heart hammered away in my chest as I contemplated my next move.

I decided to make the effort to get off the couch, so I could make my way to where the light switch was, so I could flick my lights back on. As I got up, my legs wobbled, and I had to steady myself on the armrest of the couch. I walked slowly, towards the staircase leading to my rooms upstairs.

If only I could switch my lights back on quickly. The staircase was dark, and I had to use my intuition and the familiarity of my home, to make my way to my bedroom door.

I passed by the bathroom, and as the door had been left slightly open, I could see through the open bathroom window that the streets were quiet. When did that happen? There were no sounds of excited children or their equally excited parents who had been laughing just as much as their children. The neighbourhood had gone dead.

I had reached my bedroom door now.

I could feel beads of perspiration on my forehead and upper lip.

Before I could flick on the switch on the wall, a shimmer of rainbow-like lights flickered through from underneath the door. I felt my throat tighten, and it went dry suddenly. My breath started to come out in short rasp gasps. I closed my eyes and reached out for the doorknob for only a second. I pushed the door open and braced myself for what I would find.

As the door swung open, I gasped in shock as I was shocked by what lay in front of me! My room had been decorated! Halloween style! Why? I do not celebrate, neither do I believe in Halloween and all the celebrations that go with it!

My room was bathed in purple lights, all around. Rays of light poured from four large bulbs fitted on the ceiling. There were skulls and bats hanging from my ceiling. I stood still – frozen to the core. All this was quite scary to me. However, what drew my attention was the large pumpkin in the centre of the room. The pumpkin was large and quite plump, and it seemed it would burst at any moment. A set of eyes and jagged teeth had been carved into one side of the pumpkin. I started to shiver as I continued to stare at the commotion in my bedroom.

Suddenly, a willowy figure started to approach me. It stretched out one hand, as if to touch my face. My throat constricted and I could not speak, even though I tried as hard as I could. I stood transfixed on the spot.

'You have to get out of here'. The figure said. ''Run as fast as you can! Ruuuun!'. It spoke. Just when I thought I was going to be sucked in, by the creature as it came closer and closer to me, I started to fall backwards. I grabbed the air blindly as I continued to fall. I closed my eyes, preparing myself for the worst.

*

The couch I lay on felt cold. I woke up and rubbed my eyes. It must have all been a dream even though it had felt so real. When I went to bed, my bedroom was just I had left it. There were no decorations of any sort.

*

I was on my way to work this morning.

I passed by houses that had been decorated the night before. There were fake spider webs hanging from roofs and doorways. I did not envy them with the cleaning up. There were spiders, flickering lights in carved pumpkins and a lot of other decorations. The streets were quiet, as I walked towards the bus stop.

I thought of what could only have been a dream where my bedroom had been transformed into a Halloween palour.

Then, I froze in my tracks.

As I went past the last house on the street, I saw the very same plump orange and purple pumpkin, that had been in the centre of my bedroom yesterday. It had the same carved eyes and jagged mouth.

At this point, all I could do, was run!

The End

Ingram Content Group UK Ltd.
Milton Keynes UK
UKHW040710120723
424996UK00001B/2

9 781803 814230